LOOK FOR ARCHIE THE STAR COMIC!

My first and last curl.

THERE'S ENOUGH TO MAKE A CAT LAUGH

MAY 1914

½

My Family

AND OTHER GREAT BRITISH COMICS!

Old Georgie

He's a top chap!

This is me, born 3rd April 1904.

There's always food on the table.

My mum, Violet, 36 years old.

Do as yer mam says or I'll clip you round the ear.

My dad, Arthur, 38 years old.

See a girl, wink an eye!

Uncle Teddy, Dad's younger brother.

VOTES FOR WOMEN

My sister, Ethel, 16 years old.

Ain't long afore I leave school!

My brother, Ronald, 14 years old.

He ain't half funny-looking.

BURP! POO! FART!

← Dribble

My baby brother, Billy, 9 months old.

Smiling gives you wrinkles.

Grandma Albright, ancient and grumpy!

Pink thumb! ↓

Uncle Colin, Dad's older brother.

I think Uncle Colin is about 40 years old. I don't know what he looks like, because he works as a gardener in Dorset. So he must have green fingers! Dad says we can visit him when we've saved the train fare. He's got a gammy leg because he broke it as a child and it was never right again. He must be nice because he sent me this book.

6.PM DORSET MARCH 1914

2 TWO PENCE

It cost Uncle Colin 2d – two pence! – to post my scrapbook.

Feathers are green, not fingers!

Dad borrowed this suit from his boss.

Mum and Dad's wedding

Ain't she a picture!

This is Baby Billy's footprint. If you ask me, it's the print of a little

MONSTER!

Ethel wears a ribbon like this to show she is a suffragette and wants the right to vote, like a man. Dad says she'll be wanting to wear trousers next.

6

PLAYER'S CIGARETTES.

2ND

T T T T
1/5TH 1/6TH 1/7TH 1/8TH

2/5TH 2/6TH 2/7TH 2/8TH

THE WEST YORKSHIRE
REGIMENT.
(THE PRINCE OF WALES'S OWN).

TYPES OF BATTALION SIGNS.

PLAYER'S CIGARETTES.

36TH DIVISION.

PLAYER'S CIGARETTES.

36TH DIVISION.

PLAYER'S CIGARETTES.

1ST CANADIAN DIVISION.
3RD INFANTRY BRIGADE.

PLAYER'S CIGARETTES.

2/5TH BN.   1/6TH BN.

1/7TH BN.   16TH BN.

THE SHERWOOD FORESTERS
(NOTTINGHAMSHIRE AND
DERBYSHIRE REGIMENT).

TYPES OF
BATTALION SIGNS.

PLAYER'S CIGARETTES.

CAVALRY CORPS.

PLAYER'S CIGARETTES.

56TH DIVISION.

PLAYER'S CIGARETTES.

AUSTRALIAN CORPS.

To whom it may concern — which is nobody except me!
29th June 1919

If my best friend, Tom, was here, he'd ask me why I'm writing the last page of this scrapbook on the first page. Well, it's the only page left, and tomorrow I start work with my uncle Colin. I'll have to work hard to earn my five shillings a week, so I don't think I'll have time for my scrapbook, or even my comics. Besides, I want to forget the war and start again.

When Uncle Colin gave me this book for my tenth birthday, on 3rd April 1914, I was just an ordinary boy in an ordinary family. We were poor but happy — all squashed into a house in London's East End. Then, out of the blue, a young Bosnian man killed an archduke in a country I'd never heard of called Serbia. We didn't think much of it at the time; it wasn't our quarrel. But then Germany invaded Belgium, a neutral country and our friend, and we were at war.

They said the war would be over in a few weeks. But it wasn't. Instead, thousands joined up to fight in the trenches and thousands never came back.

I'm not saying everything was perfect before the war. There was the awful time when our Molly had the measles and died. She was only three years old. I thought Mum would never give over crying. Well, during the war many thousands of mums everywhere lost their children or saw them wounded. It is hard to imagine how many. There are no hugs big enough for that.

There's nothing as awful as war. I know that now for sure — and nobody can tell me any different. They say that this has been the war to end all wars. Well, I hope they're right, but I don't really trust grown-ups any more.

Archie Albright, 1919
Now aged 15 years

Have you forgotten yet? ...
Look up, and swear by the green of the spring
that you'll never forget.

Siegfried Sassoon, March 1919

These are MY comic characters, Dumpling and Gravy. →

SPECIAL EXTRA · HOME 'N' AWAY

CHAMPION CHUCKLES!

I might think it was the best house ... if Grandma Albright didn't live with us. She washes my mouth out with soap if I tell a whopper. She also whacks me with her hair brush. THE BEAST!

Shut the blinkin' door!

I'd like an 'orse but they eats money.

ANY OLD SCRAP

I live at 33 Grove Road, East London. Dad was born in this house. He says it's the best in the road.

My dad keeps his barrow out the back, next to the toilet. When there is no work in the boot factory, he buys and sells scrap.

MY BEST FOODS

Suet pudding with runny custard

Semolina with jam

Bread and dripping

Sunday joint when we can afford it

Gravy, gravy gravy!

Hot Bovril

Hot cocoa

Learning is most excellent.

Mr Duncan

SCHOOL

I go to Mr D.'s school with my best friend, Tom, and our Ron. Ron will have to leave soon and go to work.

Do I see a dirty hand? Yes!

Thwack! Thwack!

ME!

I like school, but I don't like Mrs D. and her tickler. It don't take much to get her going.

WACKO, MRS D.!

Tom says I got to write that this don't look like → him. EXCEPT IT DOES!

Me and Archie is like twins!

Terrible twins!

TOM   UNCLE DEREK   LILY + AUNTIE AG

This is my best friend, Tom, his sister, Lily, and his mum and dad. They live in the road behind ours.

'Ere, you forgot me, you horrible little tykes.

Oops, and we love cricket!

Me and Tom like making our own comics, reading comics, talking about comics, collecting comics and playing Cowboys.

TOM'S BEST FOOD is a marrow bone because he's barking mad ... woof, woof!

SWEETS
Give me more!

← Sherbet dip

Jelly babies (not the green ones)

Humbugs ↗

GRAND BIRTHDAY NUMBER • AUGUST 1914 • THE FINEST STORY EVER WRITTEN

BABY BILLY'S FIRST BIRTHDAY AND THE FIRST TALK OF WAR!

Dad made Baby Billy a shoe doll at the factory. He's ever so good at them. Ethel's still got six! He made me this little paper one to stick in my scrapbook. Good old Dad!

Mum's cake had real butter and strawberries in it. RIPPING!

It was Baby Billy's first birthday. We had just cut the cake and were about to sing "Happy Birthday".

Then in walks Ethel with a whopping shiner. She'd been on a peace march to stop Britain joining the war in Europe.

Grandma Albright is very patriotic. She thinks that Great Britain has a duty to sort out the troubles of the world, even if it means going to war. She picked up her cake and threw it at Ethel and her banner.

Tom's idea. Well ... sort of.

YES, IT WAS! —TOM

THE BOSSY BOOTS BRING YOU THE WAR NEWS

28TH JULY 1914 AUSTRIA DECLARES WAR ON SERBIA.

PEACE, NOT WAR!

GRANDMA WAR

SISTER PEACE

Luckily it was the summer holidays or I might have been at school when Constable John bicycled down our street. He was blowing his whistle and looking important, so we all gathered round and some of the mums brought out tea and biscuits. It seemed like a bit of a picnic, until Constable John told us that Germany had invaded Britain's friend, Belgium, so we had declared war on Germany.

At first nobody said anything. All I could hear was Grandma slurping her tea, the chink of cups rattling on saucers and our Ethel crying. Then everyone started talking at once, except for Mrs Schoenfeld from Number 36. She didn't say a word. Her husband is German, so he is our enemy now. He might start poisoning the food we buy from his grocery shop, or even become a spy for Germany.

BRITISH WARNING TO GERMANY.

Germany has begun the great war,

Is war scary?

How should I know? I'm just a dog!

And the bad news is that Dad says I've still got to go back to school next term, war or no war.

MORE ALLIES

ITALY
ROMANIA
PORTUGAL
GREECE

2ND AUGUST 1914

22 GERMAN SOLDIERS AND ONE GERMAN SPY KILLED IN FRANCE.

Not just a pretty face – she can read as well!

22 GERMANS KILLED.
REPULSE OF A FRONTIER RAID.
FROM OUR OWN CORRESPONDENT.
Paris, Sunday, 8 p.m.

SPY SHOT DEAD.
A German spy was shot dead by the guard at Soissons railway bridge last night.

WAR games

1½d

THE PATRIOTIC COMIC
THE GREAT NEW READ FOR BOYS AND GIRLS DOGS!

BAN THE HUN!

LITTLE GIRLS AND LITTLE BOYS NEVER PLAY WITH GERMAN TOYS!

DO NOT WHISTLE GERMAN TUNES.

DO NOT LET A GERMAN BARBER CUT YOUR HAIR. HE'LL SLIT YOUR THROAT!

IGNORE YOUR GERMAN FRIENDS. THEY ARE NOW THE ENEMY

The summer holidays have been spiffing. We have spent nearly all our time playing war games. It's much more fun than playing Cowboys. You dig a trench and then hurl missiles at the girls. We don't let them play unless they're the Germans. They can't dig trenches so we always win!

Our best game is pretending we're the British soldiers that went to France just after war was declared. We are defending Paris, the capital of France, and are nearly losing to the Germans. Then, in the nick of time, more French soldiers arrive in taxis and Paris is saved! Dad says this really happened.

We don't play with Peter Schoenfeld any more because he is German and might be a spy!

Dad says we must keep our wits about us, so I always let someone else taste the cocoa first, in case Peter or his dad have poisoned it.

12TH AUGUST 1914 BRITISH FORCES START TO ARRIVE IN FRANCE

3RD SEPTEMBER 1914 GERMAN PATROLS GET VERY CLOSE TO PARIS.

5–10TH SEPTEMBER 1914 FRENCH SOLDIERS STOP THE GERMANS ADVANCING AT THE FIRST BATTLE OF THE MARNE.

"Très bien," I say. He says, "Woof."

Woof!

At night I get into bed with a running leap, so if there is a German soldier under the bed he won't be able to grab me. Dad says that the Germans won't kill children, but you can't be too careful.

Tweet!

I started to pee out of the window rather than risk being shot with my trousers down in the toilet outside. Then Grandma caught me! She gave me such a wallop, I decided it was better to risk a German attack than a Granny attack.

SPIDERS | RATS | BEETLES | MOTHS | DEAD BIRDS | FLIES

I haven't found a German in the toilet yet, just bugs and stuff.

V.I.D.

Very Important Document!

READ IT!! READ IT!!

Lord Roberts, a very important army field marshal, has sent a message to all the children of the British Empire to explain why we are fighting the war. I have copied it down and pinned it above my bed. Grandma says our Ethel should have it pinned to her brain.

↑ Ethel says all this is rubbish and I should know better than to repeat it, but she can't ALWAYS be right, can she?

LORD KITCHENER BECOMES THE MINISTER OF WAR.

BRITISH PEOPLE CATCH WAR FEVER AND THINK THE KAISER IS A DEVIL.

DOGS ARE TRAINED AS ARMY MESSENGERS.

A beetle from the bog!

HEROES OF THE WAR

MY LIFE IS ...

Uncle Teddy

The same week that I went back to school, Uncle Teddy joined the army. He is in the Royal Middlesex Regiment. This is a picture of him training on Epsom Downs. They had to use umbrellas and broom handles because there weren't enough rifles.

UNCLE T.'s NEW SONG

(This one doesn't make Grandma smile!)

Where are our uniforms? Far, far away. When will our rifles come? P'raps, p'raps some day...

It's just a bit of soot from the steam.

When he had finished training we went to the station to see him off to France. His hair had been cut short and he looked very fine in his uniform. There were lots of people hugging and kissing — yuk. Mum and our Ethel cried, soppy hens!

OFFICERS KILLED.

The newspapers have just started to print the names of soldiers killed in action — each day the list gets longer. I hope UNCLE TEDDY doesn't end up as a name in the newspaper; we use our old newspaper in the toilet.

It's just temporary, mate.

Where are our friends?

We 'ave none.

What about our families?

All spies!

Smelly pong Germans!

Come along, boys!

ENLIST TODAY

Mr Schoenfeld has been arrested! He has been taken to an internment camp with a whole load of other Germans who might turn into spies. They will have to stay there until the end of the war. I am now definitely not allowed to play with Peter — anyway, he has stopped coming to school.

OCTOBER 1914
MILLIONS OF MEN (EVEN DADS) JOIN THE FORCES. THEY THINK THE WAR WILL SOON BE OVER.

OCTOBER—NOVEMBER 1914
THE ALLIES AND CENTRAL POWERS DIG TRENCHES OPPOSITE EACH OTHER.

SLOWLY CHANGING!

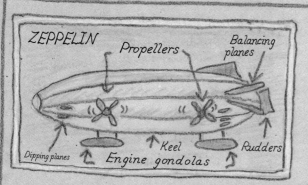

TAKE COVER!

I think Constable John should arrest Peter for being the son of a German, but he is too busy practising for a Zeppelin raid. He rides his bicycle up and down our road shouting and ringing his bell. We have to run and shelter under the kitchen table. IT IS EVER SO MUCH FUN!

Such a nice boy. He called me "old dear".

ALL CLEAR!

We stay undercover until a Boy Scout from the local pack rides through the street shouting, "All clear!" Ron and me would like to join the scouts, but Dad says we ain't got money to spare for the subs.

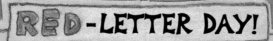

RED-LETTER DAY!

The whole family has been writing to Uncle Teddy and at last we have got a letter from him. OUR FIRST WAR LETTER! He doesn't think the war will be over by Christmas, worst luck. He has asked us to send ever so many things. He says the army hasn't got enough stuff for all the new soldiers.

Sorry about that — a bit of bully beef from the trench.

November 1914

Dear Family,

Here I am in France and jolly glad to be here, pocketing my 12/6d. I certainly get more fresh air than I did in the boot factory! It seems there were a few close encounters with the Hun before I arrived, but now we spend most of our time sitting in our trenches opposite the German trenches. In between

CHRISTMAS IN LONDON

HAPPY CHRISTMAS, FOLKS! THE BAD NEWS IS, THE WAR IS NOT OVER!

25TH DECEMBER 1914

Round the Yule log we may gather and our hands may holly twine. But our hearts are with our soldiers, fighting in the battle line.

CHRISTMAS FEAST
Hats to be worn
STUFFED TURKEY
(It was 10d a pound, but Dad splashed out!)

ROAST POTS

SPROUTS
(yuk, yuk, yuk!)

AUNT AG'S MINCE PIES
(lead weights)

MUM'S PEACE PUDDING
(so scrumptious)

YUMMY YELLOW CUSTARD

Doris! That dog's digging up the garden again.

Last night the Germans dropped a bomb from a Zeppelin airship and it landed on a garden in Dover. Nobody was hurt, but it could have killed a child or even a pet. Maybe Dad is wrong about the Germans not killing children. Tom's dad says that the Germans have made steel darts to drop on us and that they can split a person in two!

PEACE PUDDING

We didn't let the Germans spoil our Christmas, though! Tom and his family came over and we ate until we were bursting. Mum played the piano and we all sang carols and war songs. Dad gave me a whole shilling and our Ethel gave me two brilliant new comics for my collection. She only cried when we drank a toast to "absent friends". All the girls cried then, even Grandma — they were thinking of Uncle Teddy, of course!

On Boxing Day two German planes flew up the Thames and I actually saw them! They were chased off by a couple of airmen from the Royal Flying Corps. There was lots of firing. I think it is the first time there has ever been a gunfight in the air. It is certainly the first time I have seen a plane. From now on we have got to dim our lights at night to make it harder for the German airmen to see London.

The BossyBoots are on holiday...

| What do you think Uncle Teddy's doing? | I hope he got that food parcel. | I hope he's having a party with his mates. | I hope he's doing his duty. |

When we were celebrating Christmas we didn't talk about Uncle Teddy a lot, but I know we all wondered how he was spending Christmas. We hoped that he had got the parcel of food we sent him and that he was able to have a party with his mates. Then we got this amazing letter from him with a picture that he drew of the trenches on Christmas Day.

UNCLE TEDDY'S LETTER

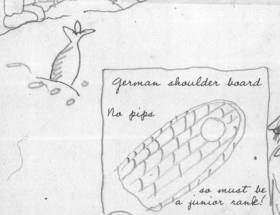

German shoulder board

No pips

so must be a junior rank!

I gave him a tin of bully beef, poor chap, but he did say he was hungry.

I miss Uncle T!

Don't miss next week's issue and their triumphant return!

Count Ferdinand von Zeppelin

This man is NOT a hero. He is the creator of the first fleet of Zeppelins.

Oh, woof! The Zepps have come!

Felix
MENDELSSOHN-

RESCUED FROM THE GUTTER – WATCH OUT! THIS MAN AND THESE MUSICAL NOTES CAN DO YOU HARM!

The New Year has not started well; the Germans have started bombing us from Zeppelin airships. It is very scary – not even Baby Billy is safe now. We have moved our beds downstairs in case a bomb hits our house and we have filled tubs with water against incendiaries.

Mrs Schoenfeld had her shop looted because she is married to a German; people are just so angry about the German bombs killing civilians.

Aunt Agatha has thrown her piano out into the street because it was made in Germany, and Uncle Derek tore up all her German music and scattered it in the road.

19TH JANUARY 1915

FIRST ZEPPELIN RAIDS ON BRITAIN

THE GERMANS MAKE HISTORY, AS WOMEN AND CHILDREN ARE ATTACKED FROM THE AIR FOR THE FIRST TIME EVER!

LONDONERS REBEL AND TURN ON LOCAL GERMAN ALIENS

NOW DO YOU SEE WHERE WAR LEADS?

What ho!

Even our Ethel hates the Germans now and has joined the war effort! She and Grandma go to Victoria Station every evening and serve tea to the wounded soldiers arriving back from the trenches. She says it breaks your heart to see some of them.

Mum and Aunt Agatha are having knitting and bandage-rolling parties.

Me, Tom, Ron and O.G. are trying to keep extra fit in case we are needed to fight.

Tom says that I'm turning into a right good artist. He is **RIGHT**.

TWO DAYS LATER

I ain't had much time to do my scrapbook. Ron's gone barmy about us being fit enough to serve our country. I think I'm too young, but he says that age don't matter, we must all do our bit.

NB Baby Billy still looks like a pig, but he's got more hair now. If we run short of food he might never ever grow any bigger.

Anyway, I think that I am doing my bit by saying this special grace before meals. "Thank God for my good dinner and for the British Navy." The government has asked all children to say it because the Germans plan to surround our island with submarines and sink our food ships so that we all die of starvation.

It makes a bigger splash when it sinks!

PERISCOPES

HATCH

DECK

HYDROPLANE

We, the great British Navy, will sink all German subs and save the nation's food!

PROPELLER

This is a German submarine, the monster that will guzzle our food.

TORPEDO TUBE

1D PLUCK

THE PATRIOTIC WEEKLY. SPRING 1915

Either you got it, or you ain't.

BUT WE ALL NEED IT!

I went to school today and the sun shone every minute.

We painted ... yellow daffodils ... to celebrate the arrival of spring.

MY WORST DAY

When I got home from school, I saw the telegraph boy lean his bike against our wall. He walked up the path and knocked on the door. He handed Mum a telegram. It regretted to inform us that Edward Albright was killed in action. Lord Kitchener sent his sympathy. So don't that make it better.

POW! ZAP! BOINK! Another load of Germans captured!

At first, being at war was like being in a comic strip. It ain't like that now — IT'S REAL.

EAST LONDON RECRUITING OFFICE ALL BRANCHES OF THE ARMY

Uncle D. Don't they scrub up well! My dad! Look, no scarf!

We'll shed the old and don the new. For we're going to see this business through.

Dad and Uncle Derek say they won't let the Germans get away with killing Uncle Teddy, so they have both joined up. I don't want my Dad to be "killed in action" too. NOT EVER.

TWO WEEKS LATER

MIDDLESEX REG.

Dad and Uncle Derek only volunteered two weeks ago, but they've already gone to France. They are in Uncle Teddy's regiment.

My dad nicked this for me from his sergeant. He's called Sergeant Harris and Dad says he's got a real bark on him, but he'll not let his men do nothing stupid.

DETAIL OF ARTICLES TAKEN IN FIELD BY DISMOUNTED MEN.

CARRIED ON PERSON.

Clothing:—
1 Great Coat.
1 Service Dress Cap.
1 S. D. Jacket.
1 pair S. D. Trousers.
1 pair Putties.
1 Brassard for R.A.M.C.
1 Identity Disc.
1 Field Dressing, sewn in S.D. Jacket.
1 Waterproof Cape for Cyclists.

1 Clasp Knife with Tin Opener..
2 pairs Socks (one pair in Great Coat pocket).
1 Flannel Shirt.
1 pair Ankle boots with Laces.
1 pair Braces.

In Kit Bag. { 1 Flannel Shirt. 1 Towel.

CARRIED ON PERSON.

Equipment and Necessaries:—
Belt, with Cartridge Carriers.
Frog.
Intrenching Tool and Carrier.
2 Braces.
Reat Coat Carrier.
Mess Tin and Cover.
Water bottle and Carrier.
Whistle and Lanyard (N.C.Os. only).

In Haversack. {
1 Shaving Brush.
1 Tooth Brush.
1 Comb, 1 Holdall.
1 Fork, 1 Housewife.
1 Table Knife, 1 pair Laces.
1 Razor, 1 Towel.
1 Spoon, 1 Cake Soap.
1 Pay Book.

Arms:—
Rifle and Sling with Oil Bottle and Pullthrough.
Bayonet with Scabbard.
Rounds, S.A.A.

I had to write this for Mum as she ain't good at her letters, never having finished school.

I loved our Teddy to pieces. — Mum

Me too. — Ethel

He was my mate. — Dad

He was the best batsman. —. Ron

I'm ever so sorry. He was a great bloke and we'll all miss him. — Uncle Derek

I'll miss his loose change too! — Tom

He did his duty. — Grandma Albright

I did this strip for Uncle Teddy cos we're going to miss him so much.

Mr Duncan let me have this paper because I said it was for something special. Paper's that short now - we have to be ever so careful.

While our men FIGHT, our women must WORK!

"My Arthur won't be short of ammo!"

After Mum had seen them off at the station, she went to sign up for work in the munitions factory making shells for guns.

"Cap or no cap, yer won't get a man's wage."

Our Ethel went to the boot factory to take over Dad's job. She is only paid half of Dad's wages.

"About time we had some discipline in this house."

Dad would be really cross. He thinks women should stay at home and mind the kids. Baby Billy thinks so too.

A | B

A. Shrapnel iron – empty

B Shrapnel iron

APRIL 3rd 1915 ★ MY BIRTHDAY

I MISS MY DAD

"Do as your Mam says!"

Mum was at work and Grandma was grumpy, so I went to Tom's house for tea.

"I got the jam out, special."

MARROW JAM ← YUCK!

Our first postcard from Dad !!

He forgot to mention my birthday, or if he saw King George and King Albert of Belgium, but I forgive him. Poisonous gas sounds really frightening — I hope the Zepps can't drop it on us.

82. THE KING AT THE FRONT.
King George and King Albert enjoy an amusing anecdote
Official Photograph—Crown Copyright res. "Daily Mail" War Pictures

The Lusitania, one of the giants of the Atlantic, was 790 feet long, 88 feet wide, and displaced 32,500 tons.

GERMAN PIRATES SINK THE LUSITANIA.

7th May We share a newspaper with Auntie Ag now because money is tight and everything costs more. There was this TERRIBLE story in it today; the Germans have torpedoed a passenger liner! There were 1,198 people killed. I can't even imagine that number; it must be like all the people in the East End. The newspaper said that 128 of the dead were Americans — and they're not even in the war!

Five men from our road, including Uncle Teddy, have been killed. Three of the men had kids.

18TH MARCH 1915
WOMEN! OUR GOVERNMENT WANTS YOU TO GO OUT TO WORK SO MEN CAN GO AND FIGHT

22ND APRIL 1915
WOMEN! THE GERMANS ARE NOW USING POISONOUS GAS AGAINST OUR MEN GO OUT AND FIGHT FOR PEACE!

7TH MAY 1915
GERMAN SUBMARINE SINKS THE LUSITANIA

AMERICA, please join the war. We need you!

BOYS AT WORK

Ron says lots of boys are leaving school before they are 14 and taking jobs as clerks, factory workers, chauffeurs, messengers, telegraph boys, errand boys, miners, builders, rag and bone boys, and lots of other things. Even GIRLS are going out to work!

Uncle Colin — WE NEED VEG.

WAR ONE YEAR OLD. 1D SUMMER Special ARCHIE'S DAD HOME ON LEAVE. AUGUST 1915. READ ALL ABOUT IT!

I haven't had much time to do my scrapbook because I've been at school.

Also, with Mum and Ethel at work, my list of chores is long enough to reach the trenches!

BUT NOW IT'S THE HOLIDAYS!!!!!!!!! Ron won't play with us much these days — he's too busy pretending he's Dad and collecting scrap — but Tom and me still have a brilliant time. We do our exercises, hunt for German spies and, of course, play trenches!

We've been banned from our back yard because we broke a window, shooting at Germans!

We've also been banned from Uncle Derek's veg patch — we was hungry and nicked a cucumber.

Food has been a bit short lately and Grandma has taken to locking the larder and wearing the blinkin' key around her blinkin' neck!

DAD WILL BE HOME TOMORROW!

Usually Dad whistles as he comes down Grove Road, so we know he's nearly home. He didn't whistle today — he knocked, which isn't like him. His uniform was covered in stinky yellow mud and he looked grey, dirty and bent. Old Georgie and Baby Billy both howled when they saw him.

Dad has lost so much weight that Mum and Grandma are determined to feed him up before he goes back next week. So there's a bit more food in my tum!

ONE WEEK LATER

Dad went back to the trenches today. He was so sad and quiet all leave; he wasn't like my usual dad. Still, I ~~cried~~ hated him going again and so did O.G.

WAR BAKE

1 lb bacon fat, minced
Stale bread
Leftover veg
2 tbsps oatmeal
Pint liquid

Mix up, pour into dish. Bake in moderate oven for 30 mins. Turn out and eat cold, with or without brown sauce!

ARRAS. The German Shells demolish Whole Houses.

FREE MEAL

Vile green slime balls!

It'll be the whole school soon.

Because of the war, lots of the kids at school don't have a dad. You can always tell because they get free school lunches. The rest of us have to pay 1/3d a week, or go without.

no coal. What's more, I've got chilblains.

HALF ITCH!!

↓

Grandma says I shouldn't complain because some of the Tommies in the trenches 'ave got trench foot. Their feet can swell up really big.

↓ ↓

Or their flesh can rot and drop off!

↓ ↓

You'd believe any old rot!

24

WINTER·1915
ARCHIE ALBRIGHT'S

SPECIAL REPORT ON
A BRAVE WAR HERO
NURSE EDITH CAVELL

1D

SHE HAD PLUCK!

Cleanliness is next to Godliness!

Aah, oui, oui.

When the war started, an English nurse called Edith Cavell was teaching at a medical college in Brussels.

The Red Cross helps all sides.

Aah, oui, oui.

When the Germans invaded Belgium and captured Brussels last year, her college became a Red Cross hospital.

Merci. **Danke.** **Thanks, duck.**

When you are better, I will take you both for my prisoner. Ya! Ya! Ya!

Not if I can help it.

Nurse Cavell stayed to look after the wounded soldiers, whichever side they were on. Lots of British and French soldiers were trapped behind enemy lines, and when their wounds were better they needed help to escape from enemy territory.

You do so much for us, Nurse Cavell.

Shhh! The Germans mustn't hear you.

Not only did Nurse Cavell help lots of soldiers recover; she also helped them to escape. She fed and nursed most of them herself so that her nurses were not put in danger. She even washed up their dishes.

Today I think we will search your cellar.

What cellar?

Nurse Cavell soon became part of a secret organization that helped hundreds of Allied soldiers to escape from the Hun. The trouble was, the more soldiers she helped, the more suspicious the Germans became.

Our Ethel told me this story. It was told to her by a soldier at the railway station. Tom doesn't believe it, but I do. I expect it will be in the newspaper soon. Then I'll show that doubting Tom!

I doubt it. – Tom

You must return to England at once.

...your life!

...my soldiers.

Nurse Cavell was warned that she was in real danger.

She was ever so brave: she refused to leave her soldiers and return to England.

YOU ARE UNDER ARREST!

Finally, the Hun arrested her.

They kept her in solitary confinement for nine weeks.

Confess! You helped soldiers return to the front ... TO KILL GERMANS!

Then she was tried and found guilty of helping soldiers escape to Holland.

FIRE!

I regret nothing!

On 12th October, Nurse Cavell and Phillipe Baucq, her Belgian accomplice, were executed by firing squad. Nurse Cavell was still wearing her uniform. I NEVER KNEW LADIES COULD BE THAT PLUCKY! NURSE CAVELL, I SALUTE YOU!

PS I don't think that Nurse Cavell's family will have a very happy Christmas this year — and I don't think we will either. Mum says there is no money for extras and, anyway, we have precious little to celebrate with Uncle Teddy dead and Dad and Uncle Derek still at the front.
Old Georgie has taken to howling most of the night, and Baby Billy whinges instead of talking. He hates our mum going out to work.

HOWL!

We won't be pulling

BANG!

no crackers this year.

KNOWN FACT

Edith Cavell loved dogs!

So I have awarded her the dog-star medal for BRAVERY.

CANIS MAJOR
1915

This is a picture of her, from a newspaper.

January 1916
CONSCRIPTION STARTS

Our Ethel says that the army is running out of soldiers, 'cos so many have been killed or wounded. What will we do if there are no dads left in the world?

DON'T TAKE OUR TEACHERS!

(Except the rotten ones!)

1ST MARCH
This is the feather given to Ron. He ain't no coward — he's my best brother!

WARNING

Do not go outside without your disablement badge! You might be attacked by gangs of women armed with white feathers.

A NEW YEAR 1916 BRINGS...
Conscription
WOMEN OF BRITAIN SAY "GO"!

FREE TODAY

I'm sick of WAR!

When me and Tom got back to school after the Christmas holiday, Mr Duncan had gone to join the army. Mrs Duncan's sister has taken his place and she's as vile as Mrs D.

COME AND GET IT!

There's nothing to choose between them.

C.O. Conchy! Coward! I'm only 15 years old. He's only 15 years old. CONCHY! Slacker! Shirker! Lily!

Now all fit men between the ages of 18 and 41 have to join the forces. It's called conscription. If you are not wearing a disablement or discharge badge, you get shouted at in the street. Or even given a white feather. It's happened to our Ron and he's only 15 years old.

I got to do it, Arch. — No!

SO HE HAS DECIDED TO SIGN UP

How old are you? — 15 years old.

AT THE RECRUITING OFFICE.

Take a walk and then come back 18 years old.

THE RECRUITING OFFICER'S ADVICE

Walking is most ageing...

RON TAKES A WALK.

I'm 18 years old now. — Good lad. Sign here!

RON BECOMES A SOLDIER.

Bye, Arch! — Your turn next.

WILL IT BE MY TURN NEXT?

You're lucky you've one son ready to serve his country.

Mum cried buckets. Grandma didn't even give her a hug. Poor Mum — now she will have to worry about Ron as well as Dad and money.

Tweet, tweet! — Your mum's a yellow canary.

She works a twelve-hour shift at the munitions factory. Her hair and face have turned yellow from the chemicals and she's always tired.

MARCH 1916
GERMAN SOLDIERS TOLD TO GO WITHOUT FOOD ONE DAY A WEEK.

5TH JUNE 1916
LORD KITCHENER DIES WHEN HIS SHIP HITS A MINE

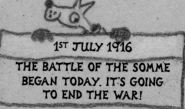

1ST JULY 1916
THE BATTLE OF THE SOMME BEGAN TODAY. IT'S GOING TO END THE WAR!

A WAR ON MANY FRONTS

Mum says I ain't got to use so much paper.

I'm not made of paper, Archie.

She's so thin now. She could easily be a sheet of yellow paper. My wartime mum. xxxxx

While Dad and Uncle Derek (maybe Ron as well, soon) are fighting in France, on the Western Front, there have been other battles going on, which the papers call "side shows". The dreaded Mrs D. drew this map on the board for us yesterday. No wonder this is called the Great War!

AUGUST

FRANCE
Albert
River Somme
Amiens
June 1916 Front Line → ← German trenches

Mum thought that Dad and Uncle Derek were fighting near the River Somme, in northern France. A HUGE BATTLE is being fought there.

It says he's going straight to hospital.

Go and see him, pet. I'll mind the kids.

Then we had a surprise. Uncle Derek has suddenly been sent home! He has gone straight to hospital, because he has got "shell shock".

This is Dad's Princess Mary Box, which he got off Uncle Teddy. She gave all the soldiers one that first Christmas. Mum hid it under her pillow when Auntie Agatha brought it home, but I snuck it out and took a rubbing from it and took Dad's notes.

SEPTEMBER

Hello, love.

I don't think he knows who you are, dear.

Auntie Agatha went to see him, but he just stared into space. Tom is ever so upset.

Shut it! I don't care if it's true – you shouldn't have writ it. – Tom

IMPERIUM BRITANNICUM

CHRISTMAS 1914

Poor Uncle Derek was gripping hold of Dad's baccy tin. The nurse said he even held it in his sleep. Auntie Ag took it off him and found two notes inside.

DO NOT TELL!

27

PLAYER'S CIGARETTES

49TH DIVISIONAL ARTILLERY, 1916

PLAYER'S CIGARETTES

28TH (COUNTY OF LONDON) BN., THE LONDON REGT (ARTISTS RIFLES) 1914

PLAYER'S CIGARETTES

24P/25TH (COUNTY OF LONDON) BN. THE LONDON REGIMENT. 1916

PLAYER'S CIGARETTES

4TH BN, THE QUEEN'S OWN (ROYAL WEST KENT REGT), 1914

NOVEMBER 1916 PLUCKY RON RETURNS FROM THE FRONT.

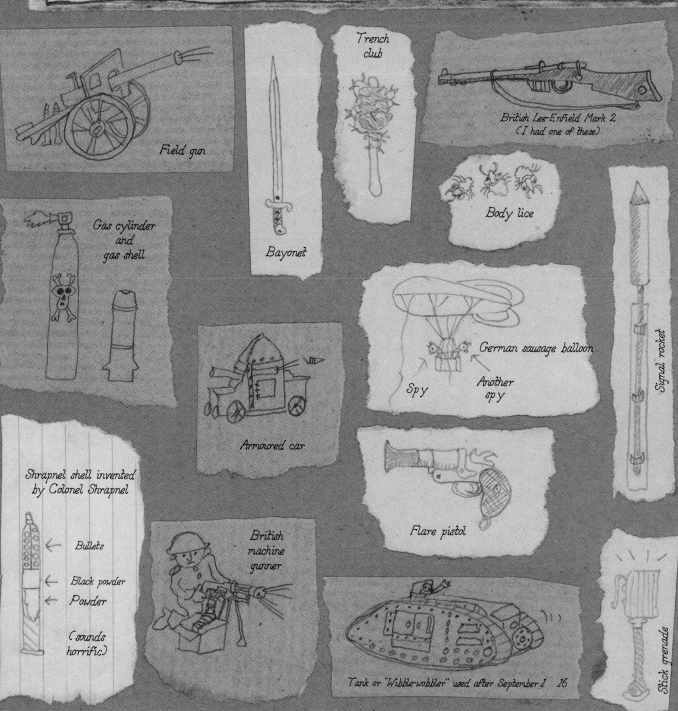

Field gun

Trench club

Bayonet

British Lee-Enfield Mark 2
(I had one of these)

Gas cylinder and gas shell

Body lice

German sausage balloon

Spy

Another spy

Signal rocket

Armoured car

Flare pistol

Shrapnel shell invented by Colonel Shrapnel

← Bullets

← Black powder

← Powder

(sounds horrific)

British machine gunner

Tank or "Wibble-wobbler" used after September 1 16

Stick grenade

Mum was right about Dad being in the Battle of the Somme. So was Ron, for just half a day! He joined Dad in the trenches in the morning and by the afternoon he was wounded and on his way back to England! The next day, the battle ended — but not the war, as everyone had hoped. Ron has quite bad shrapnel wounds and can't walk much, but we're just glad to have him home. He says he would be dead now if Dad and a mate of his hadn't rescued him from no-man's-land.

Ron has banned the Bossy Boots. He says we're surrounded by bossy women already!

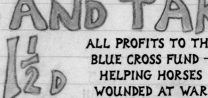

AND TAKES UP ART!

.1½D

ALL PROFITS TO THE BLUE CROSS FUND – HELPING HORSES WOUNDED AT WAR

A WAR WOUND. IT HURTS!

No, I ain't. Art is for sissies, not soldiers. This is a one-off.

PLAYER'S CIGARETTES

5TH (CUMBERLAND) BATTALION, THE BORDER REGT. 1914

French pack donkey

Ratcatcher terrier

German horse in gas mask

PLAYER'S CIGARETTES

CHESHIRE FIELD COMPANY ROYAL ENGINEERS, 1914

Messenger pigeon

French mascot

Indian soldier with his bike, in France

German hawk, trying to catch a British pigeon

Messenger dog leaping a trench

PLAYER'S CIGARETTES

4TH/5TH BN., THE BLACK WATCH (ROYAL HIGHLANDERS) 1917

The Great British Tommy, walking through mud

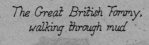

Swarming flies

Red Cross dog

Wire

Mules transporting ammunition

PLAYER'S CIGARETTES

25TH (COUNTY OF LONDON) BN., THE LONDON REGT (ARTISTS RIFLES) 1914

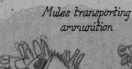

Ron seems much older – almost 18! While his leg heals he's been doing these drawings for me. Not up to my standard, but not bad! He didn't have time to get me anything for my collection, so he is making up for it by drawing me a whole load of war machines and modes of transport, including all the animals that have been used in the war. He knows ever so much about the war now. He says Dad is doing fine!!!!

Ron says he saw all these things in France – he's always told whoppers!

29

ALL PROFITS TO THE BELGIAN RELIEF FUND

YOU NEED **PLUCK** TO KEEP A SMILE ON YOUR FACE

1d

1916 CHRISTMAS SPECIAL

We didn't even get dumplings and gravy at Christmas.

No way!

Just another DAY!

I can't write much about Christmas, because nothing much happened.

BOO! — Can't you see I'm busy.

Mum and Ethel had a couple of days off work.

Those kids will be the death of me!

Grumpy Grandma retired to bed with gout.

'Ere, Ron. — I'm not a kid.

Best thing was, Mum gave Billy and me a penny bag of sweets.

CHRISTMAS IS A TIME OF GOOD CHEER, EXCEPT WHEN YOU ARE AT WAR.

Some people are still FEASTING. Ethel went up west on Xmas day with some mates. They watched some toffs come out of a swanky hotel and one of them dropped this menu. It made Ethel spitting mad. She says if there was food rationing we'd all eat fair, not just those that has money.

HEADQUARTERS
8º Division
British Expeditionnary Force

XMAS 1916

Potage Président POINCARÉ

Filet de Bœuf Tipperary
Sauce à Wilhelm II

Poulet Roti king GEORGE V

Salade

Plum pudding à la Black Maria

Fromage Whistling Willie

Fruits de la Victoire

Café Taube

28TH DEC

R·L·DAY! A card from Dad!!! It don't say nothing, except "Love, Dad"; but it means he's alive!

Xmas Greetings 1916

Ypres
Neuve Chapelle
Festubert
Givenchy
Loos
The Somme · The Ancre
Ecoust-Croissilles
Bullecourt
Passchendaele Ridge

Mum and Ethel have gone back to work and Grandma Grump is back on her warpath!

OR WIBBLE-WOBBLER AS I CALL IT

SEPTEMBER 1916
A GREAT NEW BRITISH WEAPON HAS ENTERED THE WAR ... THE TANK.

DO YOUR CHORES!

RUN!

DECEMBER 1916
MR LLOYD GEORGE TAKES OVER FROM LORD ASQUITH AS BRITAIN'S PRIME MINISTER.

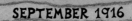

NEW YEAR'S EVE

Me and Tom will have to return to the two dragons.

1917 arrives tomorrow, but we are not celebrating — certainly not! It brings with it the end of the holidays.

RON'S LONG TROUSERS!

I wish I'd never written that. Mr Duncan, or Corporal Duncan as he became, is "missing, presumed dead". He's been awarded a Victoria Cross for volunteering to cut wire under enemy fire so his squadron could escape. Mrs D. looks proud, but so sad. I'm going to be ever so nice to her now, in memory of Mr Duncan.

MR D.'S MEDAL.

FOR VALOUR

19th January 1917 ← NOT A GOOD MONTH

Something terrible has happened, but I will have to write about it tomorrow. It's really late and we've run out of candles.

NEXT DAY   BANG !!

FLAMES AND BLACK SMOKE COVERED THE SKY!

WE THOUGHT IT WAS A BOMB, BUT IT WAS AN EXPLOSION AT MUM'S FACTORY.

NO WORD FROM DAD SINCE XMAS.

BANG!

It was 6.52 in the evening. Mum wasn't home yet, so we'd started tea without her. Suddenly, there was a huge bang!

MUMMY!

We don't want cocoa, we want our mum.

Grandma said it was too dangerous to go and search for Mum. She unlocked the larder and made us hot cocoa.

Just then, Mum came through the door, black as soot and red-eyed, but she was alive — we hugged her silly!

I'm going for Mum.

Grandma lit another lamp, Baby Billy cried and Old Georgie howled, but Mum didn't come home. Ethel put on her coat.

That's right love, cry it all out.

Even if they do rebuild the factory, Mum's never going back. She's going to take in washing to make ends meet.

31

WE GOT OUR MUM BACK — WE ARE THE LUCKY ONES!

GOOD NEWS AT LAST!
APRIL 1917 • FREE ISSUE

To celebrate the good news!

Notice that our eyes are popping out of our heads! →

I haven't looked at my scrapbook since January. Things have not been good. There's no news of Dad, and Tom's dad is no better. Mostly we just sit around reading old comics.

It isn't like my grandma to be kind. I'm scared she might smile next.

Stop moping around and get back to your scrapbook.

3rd April

Then, on my birthday (my 13th birthday!), a most surprising thing happened. Grandma Albright actually went out to the shops and came back with some PAPER and CRAYONS for me!

13!
This means I will be leaving school next year!

Well, as if that wasn't enough, three days later...

He's celebrating without us again.

6th April

THE USA has declared war on Germany and joined the Allies – WE ARE SAVED!!

Thank you, USA. WE LOVE YOU! From Archie and Tom.
WE ARE HAVING BREAD AND DRIPPING FOR TEA TO CELEBRATE.
Thank you again, USA. From Archie and Tom. Tom's allowed to stay for tea!

The American soldiers are coming here on troop ships. It will take them ages, but when they arrive, there may be as many as two million of them!

WATCH OUT, HUN – THE USA ARE AFTER YOU!!

Message to US President Wilson: bring your own food; we've none to spare.

We are not allowed to throw rice at weddings or feed the birds. Ethel says there is so little meat, the butchers are selling cat and dog meat. I am keeping a close eye on Old Georgie. Woof!

I heard that King George is so hungry he has dug up the palace flowers to grow potatoes.

British and American sailors were ever the best of friends,

UNCLE SAM JOINS JOHN BULL: PARTNERS IN THE LEAGUE OF HONOUR.

32 Yes!

Good for him!

MORE GOOD NEWS...

A letter from Dad!

He'll be wanting clean knickers next!

I don't think this letter will stop Mum and me worrying about Dad. Some people say that the soldiers will be starving to death soon and that the French soldiers are starting to rebel. Dad's letter sounds really sad. I hope he comes home on leave before I forget what he looks like. I love my dad.

All the letters sent from the trenches are censored — our dad's censor must have had his eyes closed. Lucky he did, or Dad might have been shot for treason. They say some soldiers are being shot just because they are too scared to fight.

Scared of the Hun? Can't have that. Shoot him!

But isn't he one of ours?

Help! Get me out of this comic, it's too scary!

When people aren't gossiping about soldiers, they're talking about food.

I queued six hours for a slice of bread.

That Mrs T. took two spoons of sugar. Not one, but two!

Every spare piece of land is divided up into allotments so people can grow their own veg, like Uncle Derek used to.

PEAS   CARROTS

POTATOES   CABBAGES

Has anyone grown me a bone?

The government keeps telling us to eat less food. A lot they know — any less and we'll all be skeletons.

How goes it, Tom?

Rattling good, Archie.

It ain't no comic. It's life!

Anyway, if those US troops don't get here soon, we'll all be skeletons in the ground.

NOW THAT THE USA HAS JOINED US, THE GREAT WAR HAS TURNED INTO THE FIRST EVER "WORLD WAR"!

The Bossy Boots will bring you more news from 1917, because ...

I've got chores to do.

MAY
HORSE RACING, COUNTY CRICKET AND LEAGUE FOOTBALL ARE ALL STOPPED.

JUNE
FEEDING STRAY DOGS IS BANNED.

JULY
IT IS COSTING £6 MILLION A DAY TO KEEP THE WAR GOING.

AUGUST
OUR SOLDIERS IN FLANDERS HAVE MUD UP TO THEIR ARMPITS.

SEPTEMBER
THE HUN'S SUBMARINES SHELL SCARBOROUGH.

OCTOBER
BOTH THE ALLIES AND THE CENTRAL POWERS ARE SUFFERING FOOD SHORTAGES.

NOVEMBER   ONE MILLION US SOLDIERS ARE NOW FIGHTING FOR THE ALLIES.

WATCH THE HUN RUN!

TOM'S STREET

I was sleeping under the stairs, where I feel safest, so I didn't hear the explosions. It wasn't until Ron woke me that I knew Tom's street had been bombed. Mum and Ethel had dashed straight round to see what they could do to help. Ron handed me a big jug of tea and some mugs and told me to get myself over there. It was freezing cold and the moon was still up. Where there should have been houses, I could see great gaps. The houses still standing were sagging sideways, tiles were clattering off roofs, and beds had tumbled into gardens. Ambulances were already ferrying people to hospital.

is BOMBED !

6th December 1917

I saw that Tom's house was still standing, but all the glass had been blown out of the windows. Tom was in the garden in nothing but his pyjamas. His little sister was in his arms, naked except for a nappy. Auntie Agatha seemed in a daze and was hunting through the broken things that had flown out of the windows. Their feet were all cut and bleeding from the glass and they were shivering. I put my coat around Tom and his sister and told him to take his mum to my house, where Ron would look after them. Then I went to see what else I could do to help.

NEWS FROM THE SKY...

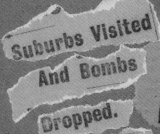
Suburbs Visited And Bombs Dropped.

RAIDERS CROSS

LONDON.

A group of hostile aeroplanes crossed the Essex coast about 7 p.m. and proceeded across Essex towards London.

AN XMAS CARD FROM DAD!!

I think your bedbugs like me!

It was a German bomber, not a Zeppelin airship that bombed Tom's street. None of us feel safe now; bombers are much harder to shoot down than slow old Zepps.

Tom's house is unsafe, so his family are living with us. Tom shares my bed under the stairs. It's a squash, but he's my best mate and we'll live and die together!

Old Georgie must have been really spooked by the bombs — he hasn't been seen since. I looked in his usual place under Dad's barrow, but he wasn't there.

Please don't be dead.

I wish he'd been here.

"HOORAH FOR THE KING"

BELGI...   FRANCE

XMAS 1917

Don't let the neighbours see you.

Although we had no meat, I got Mum to make some gravy for Christmas. I thought the smell might tempt Old Georgie home.

Come home, mate.

NEW YEAR 1918

She made gravy for New Year too, but still no O.G.

I only sells cats' meat, lad!

I hate you.

I went to our butcher's today to ask about Old Georgie, in case our Ethel was right about dog meat. He laughed at me, but he's too fat to be trusted.

The Food Controller says: eat slowly - you will need less food. Keep warm - you will need less food.

We say: your tummy will still rumble.

Stop moaning on about that dog.

Sorry, luv, just sold the last one.

POTS FOR SALE

Mum's too busy and too tired to help me find Old Georgie. She has so much washing and ironing, some nights she doesn't go to bed at all.

Ethel's just as busy, working and queuing for food. Yesterday she queued for potatoes for two hours. When she reached the end of the queue, they'd run out!

February 1918

My mum! — I'm fed up! — I ♥ you

I can't put up with these things a moment longer! — Empty purse

Washing and ironing

Grandma's stiff upper lip

Food queues — TWO ONLY

Bombs

Missing my Arthur

Whinging Billy

Not talking to my friend, Mrs Schoenfeld

Mum has had enough of London. I think that she is finding it hard to cope without Dad.

So we are going to stay in Dorset with Old Green Fingers, Uncle Colin. Hurrah!

I wish I could come. – Tom   Me too! –Archie

28th February

Mum pawned her mum's gold brooch today to buy our train tickets to Dorset!

I won't be doing no fighting!

I'm a bit sad because our Ethel won't be coming. She has joined the new women's branch of the army, the WAACS. She will be making parachutes out of silk, to save the lives of bomber pilots. She says she'll send me a bit of silk for my scrapbook.

REWARD! LOST DOG

Answers to "Old Georgie". If found, contact Tom, 33 Grove Road.

Tom's family is staying in our house in London with Grandma. Tom has promised to keep looking for Old Georgie and put out scraps for him (even if the government says we are not to feed scraps to our pets).

A PAWNBROKER'S SIGN

Our train leaves early tomorrow morning!

Dorset Special

Dad, we're at Uncle Colin's!

I am quite excited, as long as Dad's letters still get to us.

Best British.

Grandma has made us up some sandwiches for the journey.

Archie A. Wanted on journey

I have tied up all my clothes and my comics in brown paper.

 Georgie! — Georgie! — Georgie! — Georgie! — No Georgie! — They're a bit sticky.

When everybody was asleep, I went to have one last look for Old Georgie. No luck. Tom gave me a bag of sweets and swore to be my friend for ever.

MY TICKET!

GOODBYE, LONDON!   MESSAGE TO THE HUN: I'LL BE BACK, SO DON'T YOU DARE BOMB MY HOME!

THE BOSSY BOOTS BRING YOU FOOD NEWS.

GERMAN NAVAL BLOCKADES HAVE MADE FOOD EVER SO SCARCE.

JANUARY 1918 — THE GOVERNMENT FOOD CONTROLLER HAS RATIONED SUGAR.

JANUARY 1918 — WE HAVE TO HAVE TWO MEATLESS DAYS A WEEK.

FEBRUARY 1918 — BUTTER, LARD AND MARGARINE HAVE BEEN RATIONED.

FEBRUARY 1918 — BUTCHER'S MEAT AND BACON RATIONED!

PEACE

DOWN WITH THE HUN AND THE CONTROLLER.

35

Uncle C. has given me a pen-knife for whittling, so I can cut the paper properly now.

Archie says "I loves the country"

1918

SPRING IN THE COUNTRY!

MEET THE COUNTRY BUMPKINS AND UNCLE GREENFINGERS. THEY'RE ALBRIGHT!

1d PRICELESS HO! HO!

This feather is from a jay's wing, I think.

I have been so busy since we moved here, I haven't had a moment to do my scrapbook.

UNCLE COLIN

Now I know what Uncle Colin looks like! He's no painting, but he's "top brass" as Dad would say. I help him in the garden and he teaches me the names of birds and plants.

Uncle C.'s dog
HEDGER

 WREN

 WOODPECKER

 JAY

 GOLDFINCH

 WHEATEAR

 WAGTAIL

These are some of the birds that I can recognize. Uncle C. says they all have their own little ways, just like us. Mum thinks that I am learning more here than I did at school.

I ain't called "canary face" now, just "flour face".

I'm a farmer now and that's that!

Mum helps out at the local bakery. The bread doesn't taste that nice with the potato flour added, but we don't mind because the baker always gives Mum an extra bun or two!

Ron has got work on a farm, so we get extra eggs and there's a Jersey cow that gives us milk the colour of buttercups. Plus we have plenty of food from Uncle C.'s garden.

Tell your mum I had a bit over.

Topping!

Only stink bombs drop here!

Sticks is for making and mending, not biffing and bashing.

It's all perfect, except I miss my dad. I wish he could come home on leave; he might smile again if he could see how beautiful it is here. People share their sugar ration with you, bombs don't drop and there's no Mrs Duncan with her tickler!

We did have a picnic, and it was ripping. We walked to the top of Blackdown and we could see the sea. Across that sea is France and my dad. I worry that he might not make it home.

Let's have a birthday picnic for Archie.

Mum is almost her old cheerful self again.

Don't you call me baby ever, ever again. I'm nearly four.

Baby Billy has stopped whinging and started talking too much.

I'll give you 2d to go away, Archie.

Ron's leg is almost healed and he's got a sweetheart!

Uncle C. says that I was born to the country.

As for me, you can keep London. I'll stay here.

AND FOR THOSE OF YOU WHO STILL HAVE A BRAIN LEFT AFTER SO MUCH COUNTRY AIR, THE BOSSY BOOTS ARE HERE!

PEACE

BACK IN THE REAL WORLD THE WAR IS NOT GOING WELL FOR THE ALLIES

3RD MARCH

THE RUSSIANS SIGN A PEACE TREATY WITH THE CENTRAL POWERS. THE GERMANS CLAIM THIS AS A VICTORY.

NOW THAT THE GERMAN SOLDIERS ARE NOT NEEDED TO FIGHT THE RUSSIANS ON THE EASTERN FRONT, TROOP TRAINS CARRY THEM TO JOIN THEIR FORCES IN FRANCE.

NOT GOOD NEWS

FRED

CHARLIE

Twins

JOHN & JOAN

DAVE

MY BEST MATE. HE'S THE ONLY ONE WHO IS ALLOWED TO LOOK AT MY SCRAPBOOK.

I have got lots of new friends. They have taught me loads of new things ...

Expect a few cut fingers!

Never take more than one egg from a nest.

'Ere, I got a ferret and a rabbit down me trousers!

like making whistles out of hazel shoots, hunting birds' eggs and ferreting for rabbits.

Oh, the disloyalty. How quickly old friends are cast aside for new!

WE WANT OUR DADS HOME!

If the weather is fine and Uncle Colin doesn't need me, Mum wraps me a sandwich and we lark about all day. How Old Georgie would love it here. He could go rabbiting every day! If it wasn't for Dad not being here and so many of my friends being without their dads, I could forget all about the war. Maybe we will be able to soon. Uncle Colin says there is a rumour down at the public house that the war is nearly over and the Austrians and Germans want peace.

WILLS'S CIGARETTES

COWSLIP

Tom hasn't sent me any news of Old Georgie. In fact, he hasn't sent me any news at all. I hope Grove Road hasn't been bombed.

Our troops continue to be supported by soldiers from across the Empire.

US FORCES HAVE STILL NOT REACHED FRANCE IN GREAT NUMBERS. OUR TROOPS ARE STRUGGLING

24TH MARCH

THE PARIS GUN, A HUGE GERMAN HOWITZER GUN, SHELLS PARIS. IT CAN BE FIRED FROM AS FAR AS 81 MILES AWAY AND ITS SHELLS WEIGH 265 POUNDS EACH.

PEACE

31ST MARCH

WITH THEIR EXTRA FORCES, THE GERMANS MANAGE TO PUSH THE ALLIES BACK 40 MILES FROM THEIR TRENCHES. THEY TAKE 80,000 PRISONERS.

THINGS LOOK VERY BLEAK FOR THE ALLIES AND NEITHER SIDE IS GETTING ENOUGH TO EAT

I have got a new war hero. He's a German fighter pilot called the Red Baron! Three weeks ago we formed a Royal Air Force to train more fighter pilots, as more German planes were taking to the skies. The Red Baron was really young when he started flying. He had already shot down 80 of our planes when a young Canadian pilot finally managed to take a shot at him. In a flash, the Red Baron flew above the Canadian and peppered his wings with bullets. The Canadian swooped down low to try and avoid him, but he clipped a tree with his wheels. Luckily, a friend saw him and dived to attack the Red Baron. Moments later all three planes were flying a or c for

BARON!

Australian gunners, who were manning a post near the Somme. They realized what was happening and fired at the Red Baron. The Red Baron took a bullet through the heart and his triplane crashed to the ground. Nobody knows who fired the bullet, a soldier on the ground or a pilot in the air. I suppose if we knew, he would have to be my hero! The Allied soldiers buried the Red Baron with full military honours. He was a top-notch pilot, even though he was only in his twenties. I don't suppose he wanted to fight any more than Dad does. I hope the Germans are so upset to have lost their best fighter pilot that they give up fighting and let my dad come home.

I HOPE GRANDMA NEVER READS THIS!

Country CHUCKLES

Adonis Blue

For those stinging moments!
A fine dock leaf given free
with every issue.

There are stings ... and stings

Summer 1918. ½d.

I still love being
with Uncle Colin,
but I MISS my
dad every day.
PLEASE WRITE
SOON, DAD.
XXXXX

The war
isn't going
well for us.

Chirrup!

Well the veg is
still growing.

Here, Archie.

Can we stay on
a bit, Col?

Yes, we'd
best stay
a bit
longer.

I don't think we will be going back to London for a while. Uncle Colin says the rumours of peace have stopped and the war is going badly for the Allies. The Germans are jolly tough people to beat, even with the help of the Americans.

I think the war
might last for ever.

Nothing
lasts
for ever.

When the Russians signed a peace treaty with Germany, it meant there were lots more German soldiers to fight us, but we understood because the Russians were starving and fighting their own revolution! Then, last week, on July 17th, the revolutionaries murdered the Russian royal family, even the royal children. I won't ever understand that.

UNCLE TEDDY

A few of Uncle
Teddy's things have
been sent to Mum
from the front. We all
cried when we saw
them. Mum gave Ron
his watch and me this
embroidered square —
she thinks he bought
it in France to send
home to a sweetheart.
He should have bought
a dozen! My German
shoulder board must
have got lost.

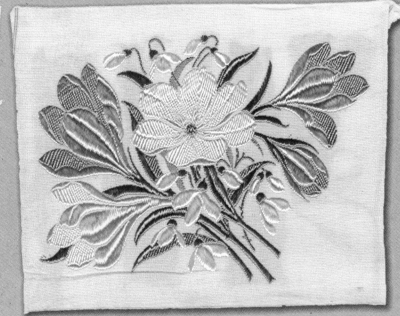

Ethel hasn't sent me
any parachute silk yet.
Maybe she's courting
a Doughboy and
has forgotten.

AUGUST 1918 — A POSTCARD FROM DAD!
Uncle Colin got out the cider, while Mum, Billy and I danced. Dad says the French means "Tender thoughts from a little girl who loves you" and that he loves us, and is thinking of Billy on his birthday. At least we know he was alive when he wrote it and if I sniff it, I swear I can smell him!

There's more wildlife than war-life in the country!

BLACKBERRIES FOR SALE

My pals and me have been making a bob or two blackberrying. There are loads and, with food scarce, it is easy to sell them.

Unfortunately it is 21st September today, so we have to stop picking them. Uncle Colin says it's the day the devil pees on them and devil's pee won't wash off!

FOX CUB

WOOD MOUSE

Soon the hazelnuts will be ready and we can sell them instead. Meanwhile we can hunt for early conkers. Besides, the war might be over soon. The newspapers say the Bulgarians want peace. They also reported that some German sailors mutinied because they were so hungry and tired. They poured water on their ship's boiler fires so they couldn't set sail to attack a British fleet!

BULGARIA SURRENDERS UNCONDITIONALLY.

THE NEWSPAPERS WERE RIGHT!

CONTROL OF ALL THE RAILWAYS.

Bulgaria has surrendered unconditionally to the Allies. Hostilities ceased at noon yesterday, on the signing at Salonica of the armistice applied for by Bulgaria.

We understand that by the terms of the p...

RABBIT

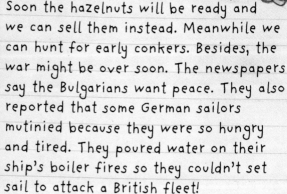

BADGER

GRASS SNAKE

3RD OCTOBER, 1918 — PEACE AT LAST

After four horrible years, Germany has asked US President Wilson to arrange peace. None of us did any work after we heard the news! Mum packed some food and ginger pop and we walked to the top of Barrow Hill in the autumn sunshine.
Ron and Uncle Colin struggled a bit with their gammy legs, but they eventually managed the climb. We looked across to the sea and imagined our dad and all the other dads, sons and uncles leaving their stinking trenches and coming home to us!

Where's Archie?

I keep dreaming that Old Georgie is looking for me in London and I'm not there, 'cos I'm here.

VERY VERY VERY VERY VERY PRIVATE

VICTORY DAY

A Soldier's Poem, 1918

It's a long road that has no turning
It's never "too late" to mend;
The darkest hour is before the dawn
And even this war must end.

Ah, his dad's back!

Ah, his dog's back!

The first we knew about the armistice being signed was when the church bells rang out. We had been hoping to hear them for days; we had been collecting wood for a giant bonfire and old candles to put in jars all about the village green. Now the day had come and everyone rushed out of their houses, whooping and screaming with joy. Tables appeared from nowhere laden with food, sweets, beer and fizzy drinks. As the stars came out, people from miles around arrived to celebrate. The bonfire was lit and the candles sparkled about us. Then, through the noise of all those happy people, the music and the crackling fire, I heard my dad's whistle.

11th November 1918!

TRIUMPHANT.

The War is over

LAST SHOTS FIRED AT 11 A.M.

GREAT NEWS! THE ALLIES WIN THE WAR!

BAD NEWS! ABOUT 8,500,000 SOLDIERS LOST THEIR LIVES!

OH, WOOF! LET'S BE THANKFUL THAT IT'S ALL OVER!

For a moment I thought it was wishful thinking, but when I pushed to the edge of the crowd, I saw him coming down the lane with Old Georgie beside him. I grabbed Mum and Ron and we ran and ran until we felt his arms about us. He'd stopped off to see Grandma and our Ethel on the way and he'd found Old Georgie waiting for him on the doorstep. I guess we will never really know how either of them got through those long, lost months. Although it was winter, we stayed out celebrating all night and none of us noticed the fall of the frosty dew.

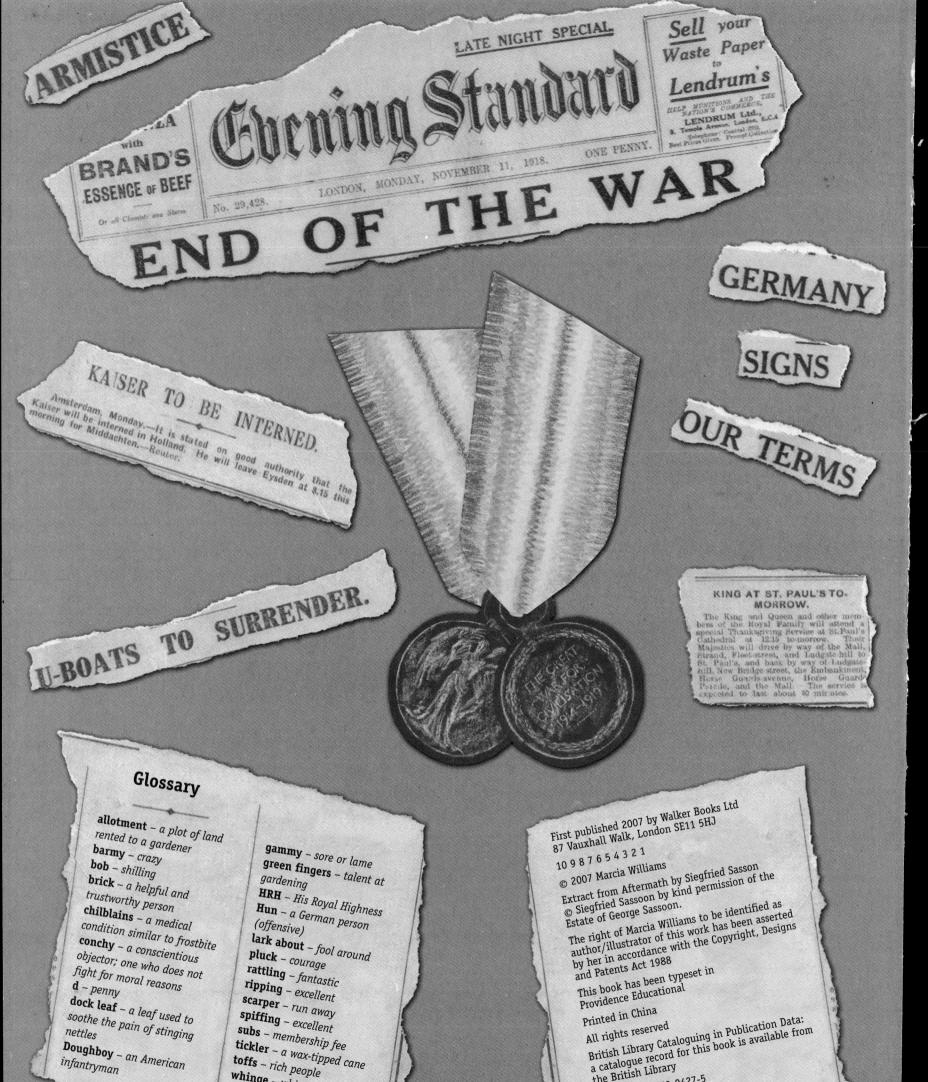

ARMISTICE

BRAND'S
ESSENCE of BEEF
Or all Chemists and Stores

LATE NIGHT SPECIAL

Evening Standard

Sell your
Waste Paper
to
Lendrum's
LENDRUM Ltd.

ONE PENNY.

No. 29,428. LONDON, MONDAY, NOVEMBER 11, 1918.

END OF THE WAR

GERMANY

SIGNS

OUR TERMS

KAISER TO BE INTERNED.

Amsterdam, Monday.—It is stated on good authority that the Kaiser will be interned in Holland. He will leave Eysden at 8.15 this morning for Middachten.—Reuter.

U-BOATS TO SURRENDER.

KING AT ST. PAUL'S TO-MORROW.

The King and Queen and other members of the Royal Family will attend a special Thanksgiving Service at St. Paul's Cathedral at 12.15 to-morrow. Their Majesties will drive by way of the Mall, Strand, Fleet-street, and Ludgate-hill to St. Paul's, and back by way of Ludgate-hill, New Bridge-street, the Embankment, Horse Guards-avenue, Horse Guards Parade, and the Mall. The service is expected to last about 40 minutes.

Glossary

allotment – a plot of land rented to a gardener
barmy – crazy
bob – shilling
brick – a helpful and trustworthy person
chilblains – a medical condition similar to frostbite
conchy – a conscientious objector; one who does not fight for moral reasons
d – penny
dock leaf – a leaf used to soothe the pain of stinging nettles
Doughboy – an American infantryman

gammy – sore or lame
green fingers – talent at gardening
HRH – His Royal Highness
Hun – a German person (offensive)
lark about – fool around
pluck – courage
rattling – fantastic
ripping – excellent
scarper – run away
spiffing – excellent
subs – membership fee
tickler – a wax-tipped cane
toffs – rich people
whinge – whine
whopper – a big lie

First published 2007 by Walker Books Ltd
87 Vauxhall Walk, London SE11 5HJ

10 9 8 7 6 5 4 3 2 1

© 2007 Marcia Williams

Extract from Aftermath by Siegfried Sasson
© Siegfried Sassoon by kind permission of the
Estate of George Sassoon.

The right of Marcia Williams to be identified as
author/illustrator of this work has been asserted
by her in accordance with the Copyright, Designs
and Patents Act 1988

This book has been typeset in
Providence Educational

Printed in China

All rights reserved

British Library Cataloguing in Publication Data:
a catalogue record for this book is available from
the British Library

ISBN 978-1-4063-0427-5

www.walkerbooks.co.uk

www.marciawilliams.co.uk